THE 13 DAYS OF HALLOWEEN

BY CAROL GREENE

ILLUSTRATED BY TIM RAGLIN

Sourcebooks Jabberwocky
An Imprint of Sourcebooks

Cover design by Kirk DuPonce, DogEared Design

Published by Sourcebooks Jabberwocky, an imprint of Sourcebooks, Inc.
P.O. Box 4410, Naperville, Illinois 60567-4410
(630) 961-3900
Fax: (630) 961-2168
www.jabberwockykids.com

Originally published in 1985.

Cataloging-in-Publication Data is on file with the publisher.

Printed and bound in China
OGP 10 9 8 7 6 5 4 3 2 1

For Jacob Martin

—C.G.

In memory of Nelle Reneau,

teacher and friend

—T.R.

On the first day of Halloween,

my good friend gave to me:

a vulture in a dead tree.

On the second day of Halloween,

my good friend gave to me:

two hissing cats

and a vulture in a dead tree.

On the third day of Halloween,

my good friend gave to me:

three fat toads,

two hissing cats,

and a vulture in a dead tree.

On the fourth day of Halloween,

my good friend gave to me:

four giggling ghosts,

three fat toads,

two hissing cats,

and a vulture in a dead tree.

On the fifth day of Halloween,

my good friend gave to me:

five cooked worms,

four giggling ghosts,

three fat toads,

two hissing cats,

and a vulture in a dead tree.

On the sixth day of Halloween,

my good friend gave to me:

six owls a-screeching,

five cooked worms,

four giggling ghosts,

three fat toads,

two hissing cats,

and a vulture in a dead tree.

On the seventh day of Halloween,

my good friend gave to me:

seven spiders creeping,

six owls a-screeching,

five cooked worms,

four giggling ghosts,

three fat toads,

two hissing cats,

and a vulture in a dead tree.

On the eighth day of Halloween,

my good friend gave to me:

eight brooms a-flying,

seven spiders creeping,

six owls a-screeching,

five cooked worms,

four giggling ghosts,

three fat toads,

two hissing cats,

and a vulture in a dead tree.

On the ninth day of Halloween,

my good friend gave to me:

nine wizards whizzing,

eight brooms a-flying,

seven spiders creeping,

six owls a-screeching,

five cooked worms,

four giggling ghosts,

three fat toads,

two hissing cats,

and a vulture in a dead tree.

On the tenth day of Halloween,

my good friend gave to me:

ten goblins gobbling,

nine wizards whizzing,

eight brooms a-flying,

seven spiders creeping,

six owls a-screeching,

five cooked worms,

four giggling ghosts,

three fat toads,

two hissing cats,

and a vulture in a dead tree.

On the eleventh day of Halloween,

my good friend gave to me:

eleven bats a-swooping,

ten goblins gobbling,

nine wizards whizzing,

eight brooms a-flying,

seven spiders creeping,

six owls a-screeching

five cooked worms,

four giggling ghosts,

three fat toads,

two hissing cats,

and a vulture in a dead tree.

On the twelfth day of Halloween,

my good friend gave to me:

twelve cauldrons bubbling,

eleven bats a-swooping,

ten goblins gobbling,

nine wizards whizzing,

eight brooms a-flying,
seven spiders creeping,
six owls a-screeching,
five cooked worms,
four giggling ghosts,
three fat toads,
two hissing cats,
and a vulture in a dead tree.

On the thirteenth day of Halloween,
I invited my good friend to tea,
and I gave HIM a present.

A real,

live...